# BRENDAN
## THE NAVIGATOR

# BRENDAN

## THE NAVIGATOR

### A History Mystery about the Discovery of America

## BY JEAN FRITZ

### ILLUSTRATED BY ENRICO ARNO

**G. P. Putnam's Sons · New York**

Library of Congress Cataloging in Publication Data
Fritz, Jean. Brendan the Navigator.
SUMMARY: Recounts St. Brendan's life and voyage to North
America long before the Vikings arrived.
1. Brendan, Saint, 484?-577?–Legends.
[1. Brendan, Saint, 484?-577?–Fiction. 2. America–
Discovery and exploration–Irish–Fiction.
3. Folklore–Ireland] I. Arno, Enrico. II. Brendan,
Saint. Legend. III. Title.
PZ8.1.F9Br [398.2] 78-13247
ISBN 0-399-23326-1
9   10

*TO LIBBY HOSTETLER*

**B**RENDAN THE NAVIGATOR lived long, long ago, when the Earth was divided into the Known and the Unknown Worlds and America was still a secret in the Unknown one. Right on the edge of the Unknown, Brendan was born, on the west coast of Ireland, which is as far west as a person could go in those days and still be on a map. Beyond him there was only the blue sea rolling out to meet the blue sky. And beyond that—what? Brendan, like everyone else, could only wonder and imagine.

And the Irish, perhaps because they lived so close to the Unknown World, wondered and imagined more than most. For certain they loved stories: fact and fancy, past and present, Known and Unknown stirred together into a grand brew. Lumps of truth there were in the stories, to be sure, but who would trouble himself to pick them out? There was always another story to be told. Even in the oldest days a good storyteller could tell a different story every night from the first of November to the first of May.

But when Brendan was born almost 1500 years ago, not only were there the old stories; there were suddenly hundreds of new stories from a brand-new religion, Christianity, which had been spreading across Europe. There were enough stories now and more than enough to go around the calendar and spill into the new year. What was more, they weren't all about the long ago; a story could be about something that had taken place only yesterday or perhaps the day before. Wonderful things kept happening to Christians if they were good enough. Miracles, they were called, and what was a miracle but an impossible story come true? So, of course, the Irish went wild over the new religion. They became so bent on being good that saints sprang up all over the country.

Still, Brendan's father, Finlug, and his mother, Cara, never dreamed of having a saint in their own family. Yet right from the beginning it was clear that Brendan was special. Didn't the sky flash white the night he was born? And didn't a neighbor's thirty cows give birth to thirty calves that same night? Sure signs these were: Brendan was *meant* to spend his life being good.

When he was seven years old, a man from the church, Bishop Erc, took him away from home to teach him how to be good. Brendan had to learn all 150 of the psalms by heart. He had to learn how to get along without eating, often for days at a time. He had to learn to obey the bishop and to keep his mind on God. And so he did. He made it a habit to think of God every seventh step he took.

But sometimes this was not enough. Once, when he was ten years old, he was sitting in the bishop's cart, reading, when a pretty yellow-haired girl began to climb into the cart. She wanted to play. But Brendan was so furious at being interrupted, he stood up in the cart. "Go away home," he cried. "And curse whoever brought you here." He took the reins of the horse and slapped them down on her.

Well, Bishop Erc had to punish him for that. He put Brendan in a cave and told him he'd have to stay there alone all night. But as soon as the bishop left, Brendan began to shout out the psalms at the top of his voice. He made so much noise that no one outside the cave, including the bishop, could sleep. In the end the bishop let Brendan out before he was even half through.

Brendan was cross at times; there was no denying it. But on the whole he was good, and before long his goodness began to pay off. One day Bishop Erc complained of being thirsty when there was not a drop of water within miles. Suddenly Brendan felt his goodness swelling up in him. He stood still and stared at the ground. Then he commanded the ground to open. And it did. It split right apart and up gushed a fountain. The bishop had his drink and of course the story got around. Sure and there was a new saint in the making, people said.

When Brendan grew up, he went on being good. And cross, too, sometimes. Especially if he was hungry or if he heard music. He hated music and its way of bursting, uninvited like a yellow-haired girl, into his peace of mind. Indeed, he hated music so much that he carried balls of wax with him and at the first note of a song—*ping!* He'd stuff his ears with the wax so he wouldn't have to listen.

With all the distractions of the world, Brendan had to work hard at the saint business. And he did. He started monasteries where people could study religion. He preached, and from time to time came up with a miracle or two.

Once he rid a village of fleas.

Once he brought a lump of gold out of the ground.

Small assorted miracles they were, nothing special that he alone was famous for. Not like his friend Comgall, who had magic spit. If Comgall wanted to break a rock in half, all he had to do was spit on it. Or like Brigit, who could hang her coat on a ray of sunshine. A ray worked just as well for her as a coathook and, of course, was far more handy.

But Brendan didn't care a whit for fame or the opinion of others. The older he grew, the less he cared. What he liked best was his own company, so whenever he could, that's what he sought. He'd go to the top of the mountain near his old home, where he could look out to sea and follow his thoughts. Days at a time he would look into the Unknown and wonder. He would squint his eyes to see if he could catch any sign of the wild places and the fierce monsters that were supposed to exist over the edge of the horizon. He would watch the sun slide down the sky in the evening and disappear. Where? Some said the golden band the sun left on the edge of the ocean was the path to Paradise. But who knew? Brendan had often thought that if he stared long enough and thought hard enough, the Unknown might be revealed to him, but the years passed and nothing happened. Even when he was seventy years old, he knew no more about the Unknown than he'd known when he was seven.

Then one day as Brendan was coming down the mountain, he met his nephew, Barinthus, who had just returned from a trip at sea. He was running, waving his arms, and panting. "Uncle! Uncle!" He cried. "I have news! Great news!"

Such a pother! Brendan waited for Barinthus to catch his breath. "Well?" he snapped. "And what news would be sending a grown man barking up a mountain?"

Barinthus' face was alight. "Uncle," he said, "I've found Paradise." He pointed west where the sun set. "Out there. I found it."

Such wild talk! Brendan sighed. "Well? How close were you?"

"I wasn't *close*!" Barinthus was waving his arms again. "I was *there*. I walked on it. For fifteen days I walked and never saw the other side."

Barinthus stepped close to his uncle. "If you don't believe I was there," he said, "smell me."

Brendan sniffed. For certain Barinthus did not smell like Barinthus. He smelled—well, beautiful.

Flowery. And not like any flowers Brendan had smelled before.

"It is the sweet smell of Paradise," Barinthus explained. "It has stayed on my clothes all this time."

Brendan sniffed again. It was a smell that could not be dismissed. He needed to think about it. So, leaving Barinthus in the middle of a sentence, he went back up the mountain. And for forty days Brendan stared west, not eating at all, just thinking. At the end of that time he decided that if Barinthus could find Paradise, so could he. He came down from the mountain, ate a big meal, and ordered a boat to be built. A round-bottomed leather boat with square sails like those the fishermen used, only larger.

When the boat was finished, Brendan filled it with friends and food. Then one fine June day off he sailed—west toward the sunset. But the boat, like all Irish boats of that day, was built to follow the currents of the sea and sail with the wind, and before long the wind and the sea were taking the

boat north. Brendan didn't argue with it. Why would he? Perhaps the boat knew the way to Paradise better than he did.

In any case, he and his friends were soon in the Unknown. And just as everyone said, the Unknown was strange.

One island they visited had sheep the size of oxen.

One was covered with birds that talked.

One island was a column of crystal with an opening in the middle and a silver roof overhead. Brendan sailed right through the middle.

Still there was no sign of Paradise. Not even a whiff.

Then one morning Brendan and his friends came upon a bare hump of an island that looked so much like any ordinary little island, they were afraid they had drifted back into the Known World. Without a thought of strangeness, they decided to cook breakfast on the island—all but Brendan, who said he preferred to stay in the boat alone. So the men went ashore, laid a fire, lit it, and had just put the pot on to boil when suddenly—*whoosh!*—the island dived underwater. And there were the men and their cooking pot and their breakfast in the ocean. The men swam back to the leather boat; the pot floated away; and of course the breakfast was drowned.

"What kind of island was *that*?" the men asked Brendan, who, being safe and dry, had found time to consider the incident.

"It wasn't an island at all," Brendan told them. "I think it was Jasconius. A whale. He's supposed to be friendly."

"Friendly!" the men scoffed.

But Jasconius was friendly. After he'd put out the fire and cooled off his back, he picked up the cooking pot and returned it to the boat.

"Which way to Paradise?" Brendan called, but Jasconius was gone.

Every morning the men sniffed the wind. North, east, south, west. But there was never a whiff of anything but fresh salt air. And then one day as they sniffed—*whew!* They were suddenly overcome by the smell of rotten eggs. They were drifting toward an island, and the stink rolled out to meet them.

"Quick! Hold your noses!" Brendan ordered.

The men had no chance to hold their noses, because there on the beach was a gang of filthy-looking giants, and they were throwing hot coals at the men.

"Up with the sails!" Brendan shouted. "Every man to his oar!"

Well, the oars went flying while the hot coals landed, hissing, in the water, and many a time it

was a near thing, to be sure. But with Brendan roaring at the giants, the boat finally got away.

For certain the men knew they were not near Paradise. What they did not know was that they were entering Monster Territory. Then one day while they were sailing along, minding their own business, an evil monster sprang up at their stern. Foaming and spouting, the monster belched great streams of water into the boat. The men bailed out the water, but the faster they bailed, the faster the boat filled. Brendan shook his fist at the monster.

"Go away home!" he shouted.

But the monster did not go away. It kept right on spouting and the boat kept right on filling up with water. It was just about to sink when, glory be to God, it turned out that there were good monsters in the Unknown as well as bad ones. A good one came along in the nick of time, attacked the bad one, and killed it.

Another time a griffin swooped down on the boat. Half lion and half eagle, a griffin is one of the fiercest creatures in any world. The poor men crouched on the bottom of the boat and said their prayers. Oh, they were done for this time, they thought. Help! Help! They were done for! But no, at the very last minute a little bird flying by noticed their predicament. Down he dropped and pecked that griffin's eyes right out.

For seven years Brendan sailed from one narrow escape to another. By now his men were sick and tired of the Unknown. Maybe there was no such place as Paradise, they said. "Oh, let us go home," they begged. "Let us go home."

Brendan became very cross at such talk. He stuffed his ears with wax and wouldn't listen to a word. It was Paradise they'd come seeking, he said, and it was Paradise they'd find.

Then one day the boat sailed into such a deep dark fog that the men could see nothing. Not the water. Not the sky. Not each other. And it began to hail. Great, round, hard hailstones battering the men, clattering against the boat. It was too foggy to see the hail, so of course the men didn't know what it was or where it had come from. Perhaps they had drifted back to the nasty-smelling island and the giants were throwing stones at them.

Brendan sniffed. No, nothing smelled nasty. He sniffed again. Actually, something smelled quite nice. Just as he was trying to decide what it smelled like, the hail stopped, and the fog lifted.

There before Brendan was a land more beautiful, more golden than any he could have imagined. And it smelled just the way Barinthus had smelled. The men took great, long, deep breaths. *Ahhhh.* For certain this was Paradise.

For forty days Brendan and his friends explored Paradise and marveled. There was not a tree that was not heavy with fruit nor a field that was not bright with flowers. The pebbles on the ground were not common pebbles—they were precious stones shimmering with color. And Paradise was big. Yes, bigger even than Barinthus had said. Indeed, they were still exploring when suddenly they were told they could stay no longer. An angel delivered the message. God had other plans for the place, he said, and they should go home.

Brendan was disappointed, but he knew he couldn't argue with an angel. And his friends didn't want to. Paradise was a nice place to visit, they said, but home was home. Besides, by this time they were bursting with stories to tell. And where would they find a better audience than in Ireland? So back they went and the stories began.

For four hundred years Brendan's story rolled around Ireland from one storyteller to another, picking up new bits and growing grander the longer it was told. Finally it was written down. Brendan was called St. Brendan the Navigator now, and his story was read all over Europe. Mapmakers drew an island in the Unknown World and named it St. Brendan's Island. The island was on the map Columbus used. But gradually as more men went exploring, the Known World became larger and the Unknown one became smaller, until at last the whole world became Known. Then how could peo-

ple believe that St. Brendan had really found Paradise? Indeed, they might have stopped telling the story except that now they found a new ending.

Ask any schoolchild in Ireland where St. Brendan really went and what he really did, and you'll hear the same answer.

"St. Brendan discovered America."

What? Before Columbus?

Nine hundred years before Columbus. The big place that St. Brendan thought was Paradise may really have been the North American continent.

Scholars, who make it their business to pick through the bones of old stories, think that some of St. Brendan's story may indeed be true. The places that he visited could be real places. In the Faroe Islands north of Scotland, for instance, there really is an island that was once famous for its many sheep (but of course not as big as those in the story). There is another island noted for its birds (only of course they do not talk). The column of crystal could have been an iceberg. The nasty-smelling island could have been Iceland during a volcanic eruption. (A volcano really can throw hot coals into the sea, and it really does smell like rotten eggs.) Tracing St. Brendan's route from island to island, scholars have pointed out that this was the same course the Vikings took five hundred years later. Indeed, it is the way ocean currents would naturally take a boat of the kind St. Brendan used.

So maybe the Irish did discover America before Columbus. And maybe they didn't. St. Brendan's

story is a history mystery which may or may not be solved one day. But if St. Brendan did reach the New World, he never knew it. He lived until he was ninety-three years old—preaching, performing small miracles, climbing to his mountaintop, looking at the sea, and dreaming of Paradise.

# Postscript: SOME NEW CLUES

In 1976 an English explorer, Timothy Severin, decided to find out if St. Brendan really could have crossed the Atlantic in a leather boat. He had a boat built like the one St. Brendan would have used, and with three crew members he sailed from Ireland to Newfoundland. (He stopped in Iceland over the winter and arrived in Newfoundland on June 26, 1977.) He didn't meet any monsters on the way, but he did meet some friendly whales. And like St. Brendan, he had narrow escapes.

In the end he couldn't prove that St. Brendan or any other Irishman really had discovered America, but he did prove that a leather boat can cross the ocean. And he did find that the wind and the sea currents took his leather boat the same island-to-island route that was described so long ago in the *Navigatio* (the *Sea Voyage*), the first book about St. Brendan. So part of St. Brendan's story could be true, even if the monsters and the giants were the work of storytellers. And if St. Brendan did not make the trip himself, other Irishmen might have. (After all, Barinthus was supposed to have gone first.) Irish monks often went on long sea voyages and often stayed for long periods on lonely islands. In any case, the unknown author of the

*Navigatio* certainly knew the correct geography, and he lived in the early 900's before anyone is claimed to have discovered America.

Only one clue is still missing in the solution of this mystery: Some relics must be found on the North American continent, objects that can be clearly identified by scholars as being Irish and from the proper period. It was in this way that another history mystery was solved. For years there were stories that the Vikings had come to America about the year 1000, but no one could be sure until 1960, when an archaeologist dug up the site of a Viking community in Newfoundland. The remains of two houses and a forge were found, a spindle and a bronze pin—all dating from the proper period and made in the proper style. So the Viking stories were based on truth and perhaps the Irish stories are too.

And perhaps Irish relics will also turn up. If they do, they will be found in the northern part of the continent. Timothy Severin proved that a leather boat does not do well or last long in warm waters.

1492 A.D.  1000 A.D.  550 A.D.